MAJOR
THE STORY OF A BLACK BEAR

written and illustrated by

ROBERT M. McCLUNG

LINNET BOOKS
1988

Published 1988 as a Linnet Book,
an imprint of
The Shoe String Press, Inc.
Hamden, Connecticut 06514

Printed in the United States of America

Library of Congress Cataloging-in-Publication Data

McClung, Robert M.
Major: the story of a black bear/written and
illustrated by Robert M. McClung.
p.   cm.
Summary: Describes the childhood of a bear cub
curiously discovering the dangers and delights of
the forest, learning to hunt and fish, hibernating, and
eventually choosing a mate.
ISBN 0-208-02201-5
1. Black bear—Juvenile literature. {1. Black bear. 2. Bears.}
I. Title.
QL737.C27M356   1988   [Fic]—dc 19   87-26126

The paper in this publication meets the minimum
requirements of American National Standard for
Information Sciences–Permanence of Paper for
Printed Library Materials, ANSI Z39.48-1984. ∞

The snow lay deep in the big woods. It weighted down the hemlocks and cedars on the mountain slopes. It drifted in the valleys. Everywhere the land lay cold and white and silent. The whole world seemed asleep.

Then a tiny bird in a beech tree broke the silence. Chick-a-dee-dee-dee! A blue jay answered with his harsh call. A few birds had not left the big woods for the winter.

Tracks in the snow showed where animals had passed. Sharp-pointed tracks of a whitetail deer going to the brook. Round, trotting tracks of a gray fox hunting for his dinner. Leaping tracks of a cottontail rabbit. Lots of animals traveled through the woods in the winter.

Other animals stayed hidden and quiet, waiting for spring to come. Under an old chestnut log a skunk lay snug in her burrow. Deep in his underground nest a sleeping chipmunk was curled into a tight ball.

Another animal, bigger than all the others, was lying in her winter den under the roots of an old dead pine tree.

It was a big black bear, sleeping on a thick nest of leaves. She had been in the den since the middle of November, more than two months before. Snuggled between her legs were two bear cubs. They had just been born.

Major, the male cub, had a white spot on his chest. He was bigger than his sister, but he was only eight inches long. He weighed just twelve ounces—three quarters of a pound. The mother bear weighed more than four hundred times that much!

Neither Major nor his sister looked at all like their mother. They had very little hair on their bodies. Their eyes were closed, and their ears were small and flat. They did not have any teeth. They were tiny and helpless.

Major snuggled against his mother's thick fur, and squirmed and whimpered and snoozed. He nursed and slept, and nursed some more. So did his sister.

Sometimes the mother bear would blink sleepily at the cubs, and lick them with her tongue. Mostly, however, she just slept.

When Major was forty days old, he weighed a little over two pounds, almost three times as much as when he was born. He had cut tiny milk teeth by this time, and his eyes had opened, brown and sparkling. Soon his sister opened her eyes too. The cubs began to crawl about the den.

By the end of March, when he was two months old, Major was as big as a large rabbit. He became quite active and started to walk, with clumsy, awkward steps.

Warm spring rains were beginning to melt the snow around the entrance to the den. Sometimes a ray of sunlight beamed in on the bears. One day Major swatted at a sunbeam with his paw, and started to follow it out of the den. His mother picked him up, taking his whole head very gently in her jaws. She put him back in the middle of the nest. It was not yet time to leave the den.

By the middle of April Major and his sister each weighed almost seven pounds. Their fur was thick and dark and woolly. They romped and wrestled all over the den, tumbling over their patient mother's back.

One morning the mother bear sat up and yawned. She went to the den entrance and looked out. She sniffed the air and then stepped outside, grunting to the cubs to follow her. Major clambered out through the entrance first, and his sister followed.

Outside was a strange new world for the cubs. Major blinked his eyes in the bright, dappled sunshine. He looked at the great tree trunks that towered toward the sky.

He sniffed at a patch of snow in a shady spot and touched it with his paw. It was cold and wet. He rolled in the whiteness, scattering it. Then the breeze whirled some dead leaves in his face. Major whoofed with surprise and scampered back to his mother's side.

Slowly their mother led Major and his sister down the slope. Major explored the woods and romped with his sister until they both were tired. That night the bears returned to the den to sleep. Soon they abandoned the den, however, and slept on beds of leaves in thickets.

The spring days passed quickly in the big woods. The cubs played, while their mother spent most of her time looking for food. She rooted among the leaves for tiny bulbs of spring beauty. She grubbed in the swamps for the juicy roots of skunk cabbage and other plants. Bears eat many different kinds of food. They fill up on whatever is easiest to get at any season.

Sometimes Major teased his mother. She was usually quite patient, but one day Major annoyed her while she was trying to sleep. He nipped at her heels, rolling his eyes and growling furiously. He pulled at her ears.

His mother roused herself and grumbled at him, warning him to stop. Major paid no attention. Running behind her, he grabbed her stumpy tail in his sharp teeth and tugged as hard as he could. Then his mother sprang up with a growl. She cuffed him hard with her shaggy paw and sent him spinning away from her. He must learn to obey!

The old bear was strict, but she was a good mother. She kept a sharp lookout for danger as they wandered, and taught the cubs to stay close to her. Their curiosity might get them into trouble, for they had much to learn.

Major was curious about all the strange new sights and sounds of the forest. He became accustomed to the chorus of bird calls at dawn, and the shrill cries of chipmunks during the day. He grew used to the sound of toads trilling in the lowlands at dusk.

He had never seen a toad, however.

One day Major found a strange little animal with round golden eyes. He sniffed at it, and touched it cautiously with his paw. He did not know that it was a toad.

The toad crouched low and blinked its eyes. Major touched it again.

Hop!

The toad sprang into the air and landed two feet away. Major was so surprised that he flipped over in a backward somersault. His curiosity had not hurt him this time.

Another time he was not so fortunate. He was lagging behind his mother one evening, investigating a hollow log, when he heard a strange sound behind him. A clumsy-looking animal was climbing down a tree. It was a porcupine.

When Major walked toward it, the porcupine grunted and rattled its quills. Major

crept closer. Maybe it wanted to play. He stretched out his paw to touch it.

The porcupine hunched up and slapped Major's paw with its tail, leaving three sharp spines there. Major yowled with pain and ran to his mother. Luckily, the spines had not gone far into his paw. He pulled them out with his teeth, whimpering with each tug.

April passed into May. Brown beech buds unfurled into pleated green leaves, and dogwood bloomed in the woods.

Major and his sister played together every day. They wrestled and growled fiercely at each other. They hid behind trees and pounced at each other as if playing hide-and-seek.

Sometimes Major played too roughly to suit his sister. Then the little female would spring onto a tree trunk and climb quickly upward. Major would follow, trying to catch her. Their sharp claws made them expert climbers.

Major's mother often sent the cubs up into a tree if she had to leave them for any reason, or if anything unknown threatened. She knew that they were safer among the branches than on the ground. She taught the cubs to stay there until she called them down.

The cubs had lots of adventures in the trees. One day Major found a nest with eggs in it. He broke the shells and lapped up the eggs.

Another time he discovered a hole far up on the trunk of a great old beech tree. He smelled an animal in the hole, and he heard whimpering sounds down in the darkness. Suddenly a furry masked face popped out. Round black eyes blinked into his. It was a mother raccoon that had babies down in the hole. She snarled at Major and nipped the end of his nose.

Major howled with surprise. He shinnied down the trunk as fast as he could go. He was in such a hurry that he tumbled down the last twenty feet. The fall did not hurt him, but his mother cuffed him for coming down before she had called him.

Eating and sleeping, playing and learning, the cubs wandered far and wide through the big woods with their mother. During rainstorms, the bears took shelter under ledges of overhanging rocks or against fallen tree trunks.

They often took naps during the day, curled up in a thicket. They slept at night, too, but sometimes they hunted by moonlight. The old bear did most of her hunting during the day, however.

One afternoon the mother bear found a big anthill in a clearing and broke it open with one sweep of her big paw. Major watched as hundreds of ants came spilling out in every direction. His mother smacked her lips and

licked up the ants with her long pink tongue. Major sniffed curiously at the little black insects, and sampled several of them. Later on he would learn to like them, but right now his mother's milk tasted better.

That evening the old bear led the cubs into
a valley where a stream flowed. Major's mother
waded into the stream. She reared on her hind
legs and peered intently into the shallow water.

Suddenly Major saw her lunge forward and
strike at the water with her paw. Down went
her head. When she rose, she had a big, fat
fish flopping in her jaws. It was a sucker that
had come upstream in early spring to lay its
eggs. She ate it, and scooped out another one.

Major saw a fish swimming right near the bank. He leaned over to hit it with his paw. Splash! He fell into the water. It was cold!

Grumbling with discomfort, Major scrambled out onto the bank. He was soaking wet and bedraggled. He shook himself off and began to lick his fur. Major was not yet big enough to catch fish.

By the middle of May, trillium nodded in the woodlands and Mayflowers covered the hillsides with green umbrellas. Major and his sister were growing bigger and stronger every day. Major's thick woolly fur was almost black, but his sister's coat was brown. Brown-colored bears are often called cinnamon bears.

Early one evening in June the old bear took the cubs down a mountain slope to a small lake. Frogs croaked among the water lilies, and muskrats swam through the cattails near the

shore. Far out on the water a loon called its lonesome cry.

The female cub stayed close to her mother, who started to hunt for frogs. Major, however, lumbered after a wood duck that whistled into the air in front of him.

In a moment thick bushes hid his mother
from him. He looked around him. The duck
had gone, flying high over the treetops.

Then Major heard a sound of splashing in
the water. He rose on his haunches to see what
it was. A strange creature, walking upright
and carrying a long rod, was coming around a
bend in the lake. It was a man with a fishing

pole. When the man saw Major, he started to climb up the bank toward him. He wanted to catch Major.

Major whoofed in alarm. He looked around for his mother, but she was not in sight. The man was running toward him now. Major squealed with fright and crashed into the bushes to escape.

Suddenly his mother was beside him. Snorting angrily, she cuffed him sharply with her paw. She whoofed, warning him to get into a tree with his sister for safety. Then she turned to face the man.

From high in the branches Major watched, as his mother ran several steps toward the man. Then she stopped. She curled back her lips and champed her jaws together, making sharp clicking sounds with her teeth. She was afraid of the man, but she was trying to scare him, too, so that he would go away.

The man stopped and watched her from a safe distance. Then he took a step forward. Major's mother made another rush at him. The man stopped again. Then he backed away and finally disappeared. He knew that a mother bear with cubs can be very dangerous.

By the end of June, Major weighed twelve pounds, and his sister weighed one pound less. They were growing up. The mother bear's old fur was coming out in patches these days. It hung from her back in shreds and tatters. She spent a lot of time scratching her back on rough logs and stumps. She wallowed in the dust and took mud baths, too.

She often took the cubs down to the lake. Major and his sister played in the water and learned how to swim in the shallow pools. The cool water felt good on hot days.

One afternoon the bear family met another bear on a hillside. He was a fine big male, much larger than Major's mother. The strange bear started toward them.

The mother bear quickly lumbered between Major and his sister and the big bear. She snorted, warning the cubs to get into a tree. Obediently they climbed high among the branches of a white oak and looked down curiously at the stranger.

The male bear grunted softly and advanced toward their mother. It looked as though he wanted to be friends. But the female bear would have nothing to do with him. She snarled and ran away when he came near. The stranger stopped and sat down for a moment. Then he started toward her again. Major's mother turned and growled fiercely at him. Discouraged, the big bear finally went away.

Major's mother had not wanted the big bear to come near Major and his sister. A male bear will sometimes harm small cubs.

It was midsummer now. Milkweed and mullein bloomed on the hillsides, and the weather was hot and sultry. Major's mother did not let the cubs nurse as often as they used to. She was starting to wean them. By watching the old bear, the cubs learned little by little how to find food and to eat the same things she did.

All through the late summer and early fall, the bears gobbled down ripe blackberries and wild cherries in the mountain meadows. They pounced on fat crickets and field mice in the clearings. In the woods they clawed through rotten logs for soft white beetle grubs. Once Major's mother killed a young woodchuck, and they feasted on fresh meat.

One moonlit night in August the bears wandered down to a cornfield at the edge of the woods. They pulled down the heavy, rustling stalks and ate the white, juicy kernels of corn. Crickets chirped around them, and an owl hooted nearby. Then Major heard a dog barking in the distance.

His mother whoofed in alarm as the sound became louder. She started running for the woods, with Major and his sister beside her. The dog had seen them now, and was coming fast. The old bear sent the cubs scurrying up into a big sugar maple. The dog, baying with excitement, leaped at Major's hindquarters as he scrambled upward. Major tumbled to the ground, squealing with terror.

In a flash the old bear was by his side. Growling fiercely, she struck at the dog with her paw. Her sharp claws just grazed the dog's side, and he leaped away, yelping.

Then Major heard a shout. A man with a gun was running through the cornfield. Major's mother heard the man too. When the dog came at her again, she stood on her haunches and struck with all her force. The blow caught the dog on the side and spun him

ten feet through the air. He howled with pain, and limped away.

The man was very near now. Quickly the old bear called Major's sister out of the tree, and together the bears scooted for the underbrush as fast as they could go.

Whang! Major jumped at the sudden sound of the gun. *Whang! Whang!* His mother screamed. A bullet had grazed her shoulder, but she kept running beside the cubs.

The bears did not stop until they were miles away, deep in the big woods. At last they were safe.

Fall came, with chilly nights. Wild geese honked overhead. Major's coat became sleek and shiny, for long, straight guard hairs had grown in, covering his woolly fur. He had his winter coat.

With the coming of frost, the trees changed color. Sugar maples flamed orange and red against the dark evergreens, while birches and beeches glowed yellow.

Major stuffed himself these days as if he could never get enough to eat. He and his sister still nursed occasionally, but they gorged themselves on ripening wild apples and grapes, too. They wolfed down lots of acorns and beechnuts.

By late October Major weighed more than fifty pounds. He now had a heavy layer of fat underneath his skin. The fat would tide him through the winter, when he would no longer eat.

One morning the first snowflakes fell. It was time for the bears to den up for the winter. For several days they searched for a good winter shelter. As the bears walked through the snow, their feet left broad tracks. A bear walks on the bottom of his whole foot, just as a human being does. Some animals, such as dogs and cats, horses, cows, and deer, walk on their toes.

Finally Major and his mother and sister found a dry cavity under a ledge of rock, overhung by thick branches of cedar. The mother bear scooped dried leaves into the cavity, making a soft bed. Then they all curled up together in the nest. Major yawned and shook his head. Soon he was fast asleep.

All winter long the snow lay thick on the cedar branches—a sheltering wall over the den. Inside, Major was warm and dry.

Some animals, such as woodchucks and certain bats, sleep during the winter in a very deep sleep which is called hibernation. When

an animal hibernates, its temperature drops and its body feels cold. Its breathing and heartbeat are very much slower than usual.

Major's sleep was not like this. He breathed regularly four or five times a minute, and his heartbeat was nearly normal. Sometimes he woke up. Then he would grumble and turn around before going back to sleep.

The cold months passed—December, January, February, March. Major slept on.

Then April came, and the rains melted the
snow. Bloodroot bloomed among the dried
leaves. Major and his mother and sister came
out and took up their wandering life again.

One day in June they met a big male bear,
like the one they had seen the summer before.
Major's mother did not chase the male bear
away this time. She went over to greet him,
and then disappeared with him into the woods,

leaving the cubs behind. Major's mother had joined her mate. Seven months later she would have cubs again.

Major and his sister were on their own, but they were able to look after themselves.

All that summer and fall the two young bears roamed the woods and hillsides together. They hunted for food and explored the woods. They played and slept and grew. Twice they had to run before forest fires and find safety in the waters of the lake.

When they began to shed their fur, they scratched their backs on logs and took dust baths. Sometimes they met other bears doing the same things.

One day they found a deserted cabin in a clearing by the lake. Major tried to open the cabin door with his claws, but it was tightly shut. Then he pried at the boards covering the windows. At last they came loose, with loud crackling sounds. Major and his sister crawled inside.

They explored the cabin from one end to the other. They pulled the blankets off the bunks and romped in them. They pushed all the containers off the pantry shelves.

Major found a big jug and tugged at the cork with his sharp teeth. When it came out at last with a loud pop, Major fell over back-

ward, with the cork in his mouth. Thick, dark molasses seeped out of the jug. The bears licked up every bit of it.

Then Major climbed onto the bureau, and it fell over with a loud crash. Whoofing with excitement, he and his sister scrambled out through the cabin window and ran away.

One day they came to a great fallen hemlock tree in the forest. Many bees were going in and out of a tiny hole in its trunk. They made a deep humming sound. The hemlock was the home of a swarm of wild bees.

Major climbed quickly up on the great slanting trunk. He ripped at the opening with his claws, making it larger. The humming noise became an angry roar as great swarms of bees

came buzzing out of the hole. Major thrust in his paw, scooped out the honeycomb, and began to eat it. The bees landed all over him and tried to sting him, but Major was protected by his thick fur.

Soon his sister was beside him, eating the sweet honey too. Several bees stung Major on his tender nose. He squealed, but he went right on eating honey!

When the leaves began to fall, Major and his sister each weighed more than a hundred pounds. For almost two years, while they were growing up, they had been together. But when it was time to den up for the winter, they separated. The next summer, Major wandered through the woods by himself.

One sunny morning in late June of the following year, Major ambled slowly along one of the narrow paths that bears often use for going through the woods. He came to a tree with many scratches on it—marks made by other bears that had passed.

Major sniffed at the tree to find out what bears had been there recently. He stood as high as he could reach and scratched his own claw marks on the trunk—almost six feet up. Then he wandered on, rumbling lazily to himself.

In his fourth year, Major was big and rangy.
He weighed more than two hundred pounds.
In the years ahead he would grow to weigh
nearly twice that much. Bears can live a long
time—up to twenty years or more.

In a little clearing he met a female bear.
Major whoofed a greeting, and touched noses
with her to get acquainted. He romped with
her for a while, and then they hunted together
for mice. The sleek female bear was very
friendly.

Suddenly Major heard a loud, threatening snarl behind him. Another male bear was coming toward him. The intruder challenged Major with another menacing growl. He wanted the female bear for himself.

Major whirled to face his rival. The other bear charged at him, and knocked Major over with a blow of his big paw. Major roared with anger and lunged back. His sharp teeth opened a long gash in the enemy's neck.

The next moment they were fighting at close quarters—wrestling, twisting, rolling over and over on the ground. The clearing echoed with their snarls and screams, as their sharp claws and teeth ripped and slashed at each other. Soon both Major and his rival were bleeding from many cuts.

Major was tiring. He was the quicker of the two, but the other bear was slightly bigger than he was. When the other bear lunged for him again, Major desperately clamped his jaws on the enemy's gashed neck. He ground his teeth together, biting deeper and deeper. Screaming with pain, the other bear tore loose and ran. He had had enough.

Major followed him for a short distance. He growled a warning to the other bear to keep going. Then he stopped and sat down to lick his wounds.

The female bear came over to him. She made a soft, gentle noise deep in her throat. Then she began to help him lick his cuts.

Major had found a mate, and he had fought for her. The female licked his face gently, and nudged him with her paw. After a while the two bears disappeared into the woods together.

McClung, Robert M.
   Major : the story of a black bear /
written and illustrated by Robert M.
McClung. -- Hamden, Conn. : Linnet
Books, 1988, c1956.
   64 p. : ill. ; 22 cm.
   Summary: Describes the childhood of a
bear cub curiously discovering the
dangers and delights of the forest,
learning to hunt and fish, hibernating,
and eventually choosing a mate.
   ISBN 0-208-02201-5 (alk. paper)

   1. Black bear--Juvenile fiction.   2.
Bears--Juvenile fiction.   I. Title

6868026   GAPAxc   87-26126r87